W9-BAG-789

My 1ST
GRAPHIC
NOVEL

THE
KICKBALL
KIDS

My First Graphic Novels are published by Stone Arch Books,
A Capstone Imprint
151 Good Counsel Drive, P.O. Box 669
Mankato, Minnesota 56002
www.capstonepub.com

Copyright © 2009 by Stone Arch Books

All rights reserved. No part of this publication may be reproduced
in whole or in part, or stored in a retrieval system, or transmitted in any
form or by any means, electronic, mechanical, photocopying, recording,
or otherwise, without written permission of the publisher.

Library of Congress Cataloging-in-Publication Data
Meister, Cari.
    The Kickball Kids / by Cari Meister; illustrated by Julie Olson
    p. cm. — (My First Graphic Novel)
    ISBN 978-1-4342-1294-8 (library binding)
    ISBN 978-1-4342-1410-2 (pbk.)
    1. Graphic novels. [1. Graphic novels. 2. Kickball—Fiction.] I. Olson, Julie, 1976–
ill. II. Title.
PZ7.7.M45Ki 2009
[E]—dc22
                                    2008031969

Summary: Kyle's team is ready for the kickball tournament. They have
practiced kicking, catching, and running. Find out how Kyle's team
does in the big tournament.

Art Director: Heather Kindseth
Graphic Designer: Hilary Wacholz

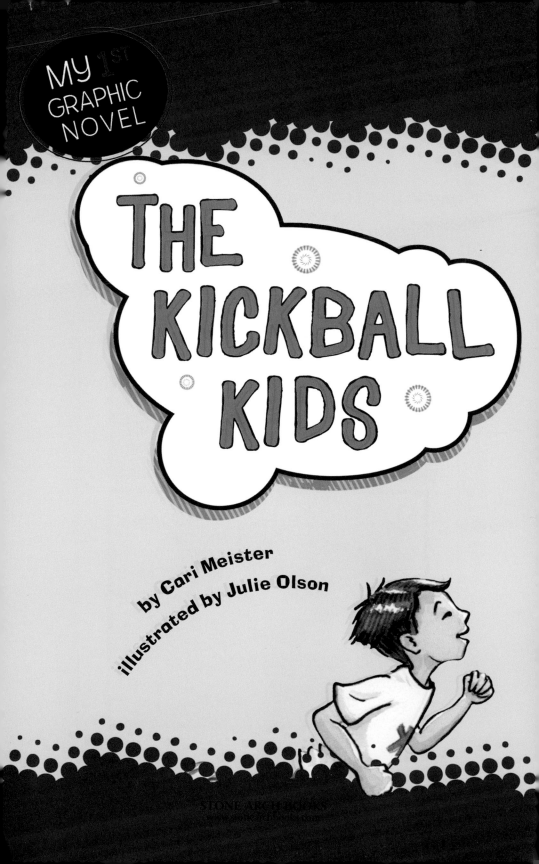

My 1ST GRAPHIC NOVEL

THE KICKBALL KIDS

by Cari Meister

illustrated by Julie Olson

STONE ARCH BOOKS
www.stonearchbooks.com

HOW TO READ A GRAPHIC NOVEL

Graphic novels are easy to read. Boxes called panels show you how to follow the story. Look at the panels from left to right and top to bottom.

Read the word boxes and word balloons from left to right as well. Don't forget the sound and action words in the pictures.

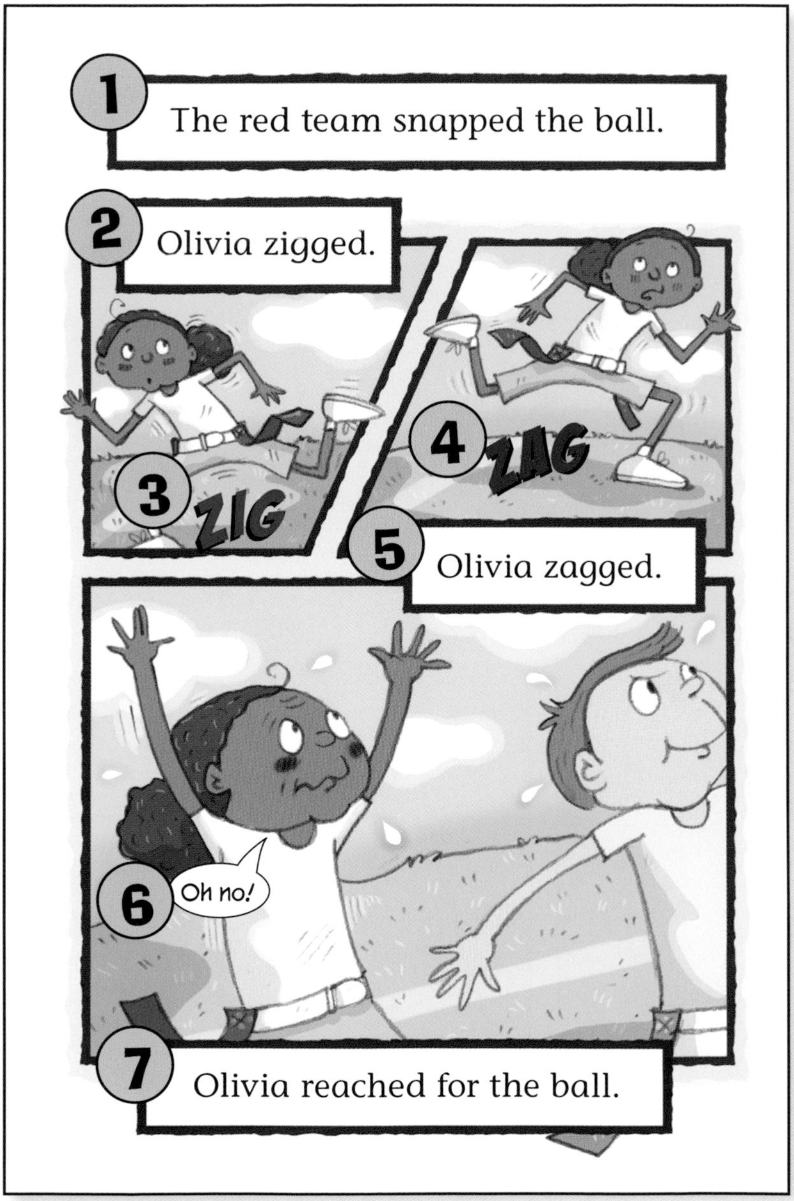
1
The red team snapped the ball.
2
Olivia zigged.
3
ZIG
4
ZAG
5
Olivia zagged.
6
Oh no!
7
Olivia reached for the ball.

The pictures and the words work together to tell the whole story.

Every Saturday, Kyle and his friends met at the park.

They didn't swing. They didn't slide.

They didn't climb.

Instead, they played kickball.

Kyle was the captain. His team was called the Kicking Kids.

They practiced kicking.

They practiced catching.

They practiced running.

Kyle watched his team.

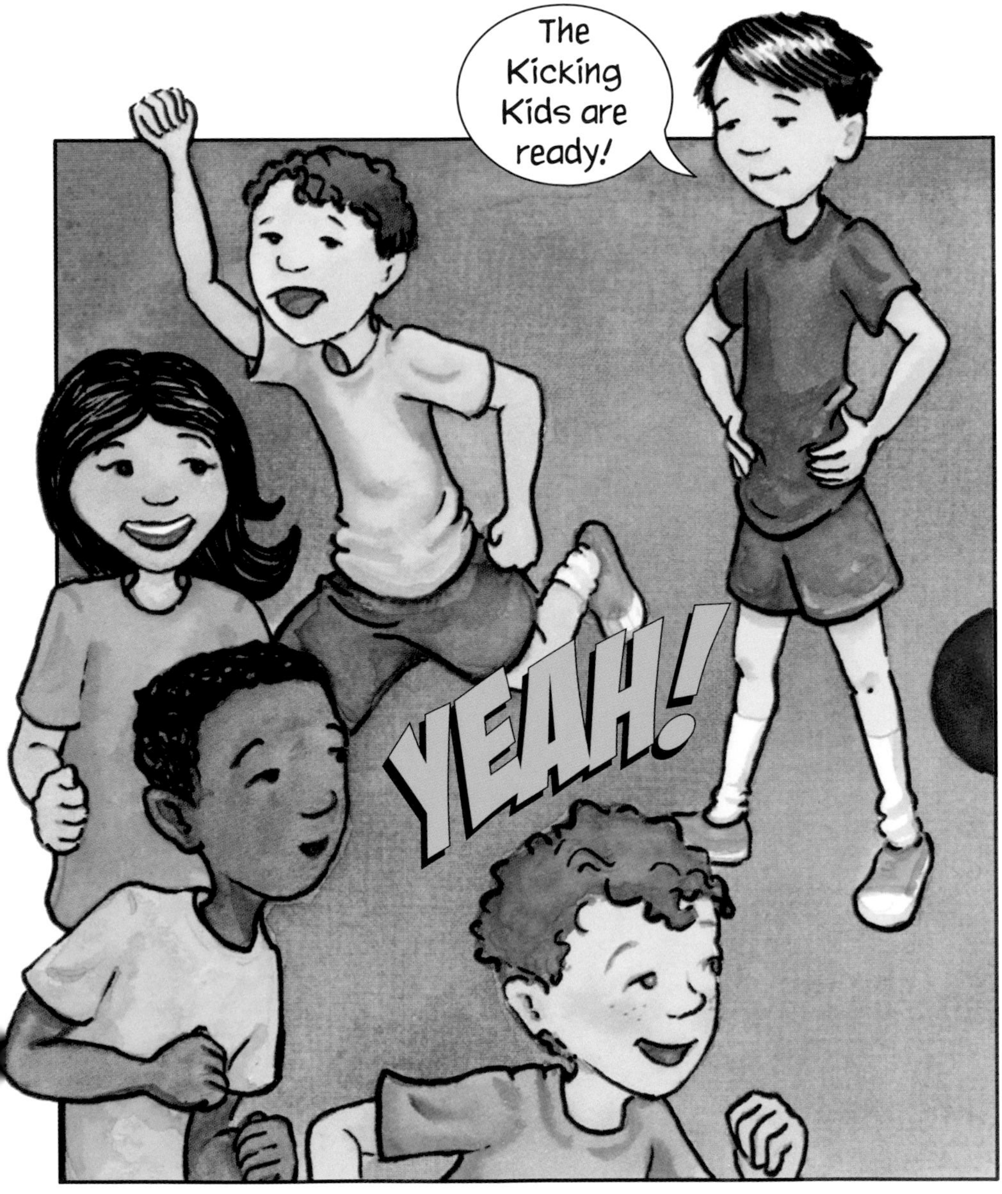
The Kicking Kids are ready!
YEAH!

Kyle made the call. He entered the Kicking Kids in the town kickball tournament.

The Kicking Kids were the youngest team. But they were good. They beat team after team.

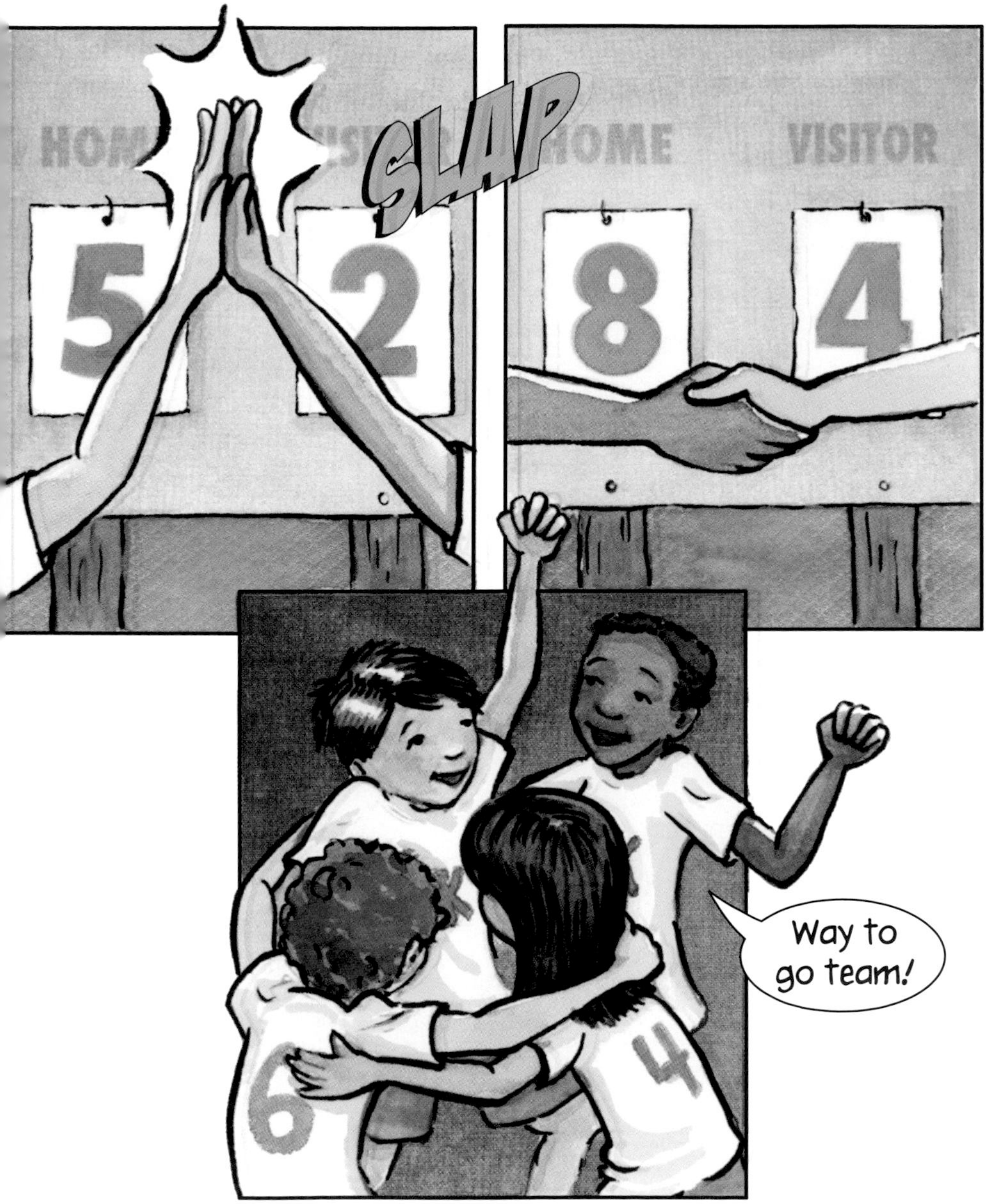
HOME
VISITOR
5
2
SLAP
HOME
VISITOR
8
4
6
4
Way to go team!

At the end of the day, they were in the finals. They had to play the Super Sharks.

The Sharks rule!

The Sharks were a team of fifth graders.

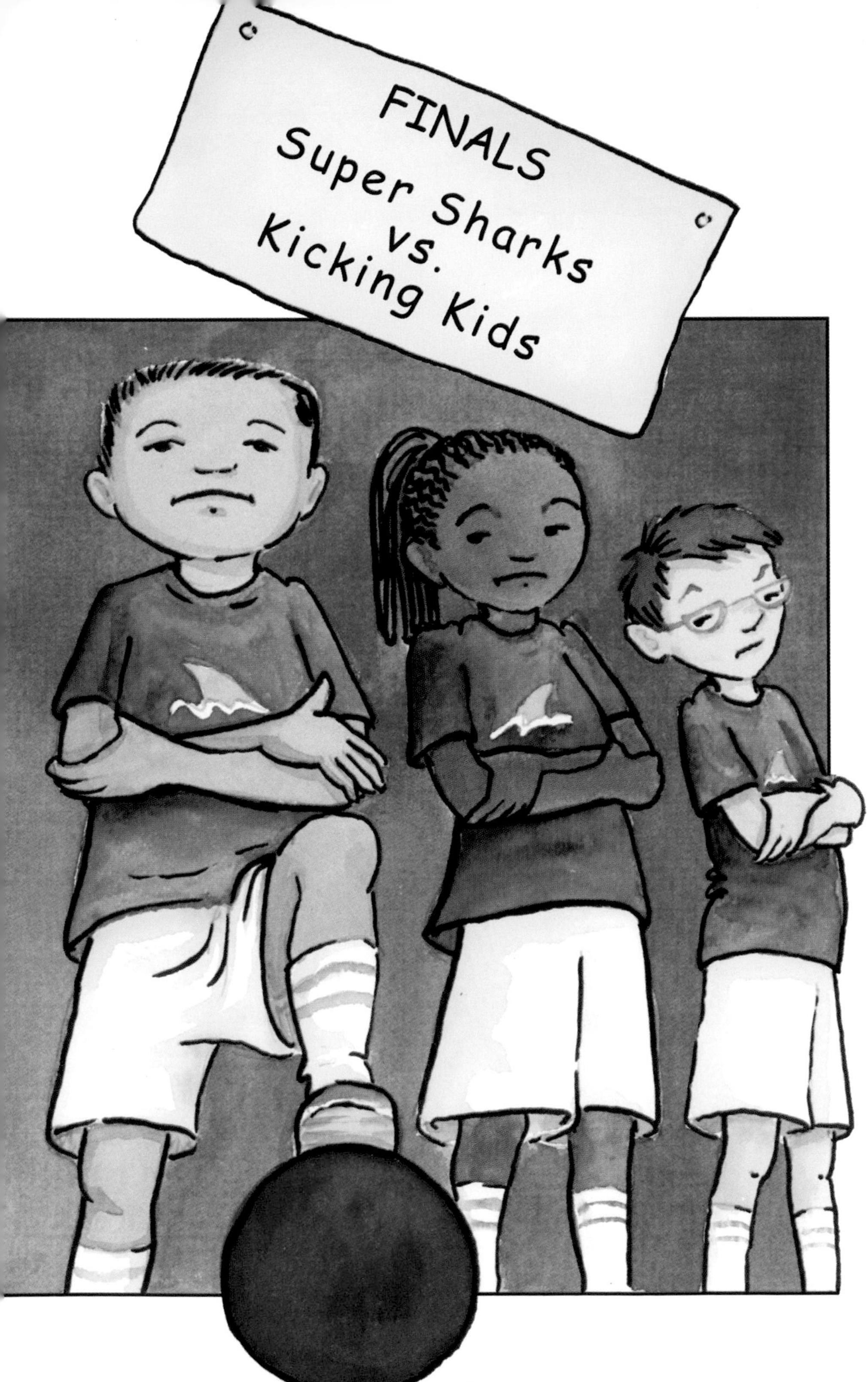
FINALS
Super Sharks
vs.
Kicking Kids

The game went fast. By the final inning, the game was tied. The Kicking Kids were up last.

Selena stepped up to the plate.

She kicked the ball
and ran fast.

KICK!

She was safe
at first base.

Jack was up next.

Jack kicked.

Foul!

The second ball rolled in.
Jack kicked it hard.

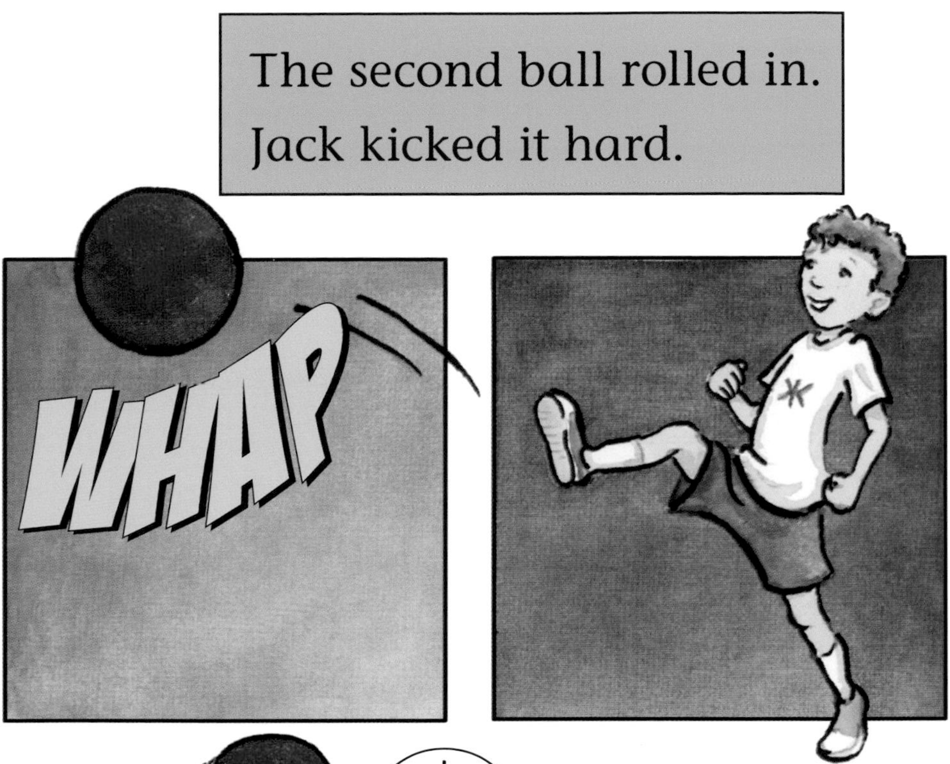
WHAP

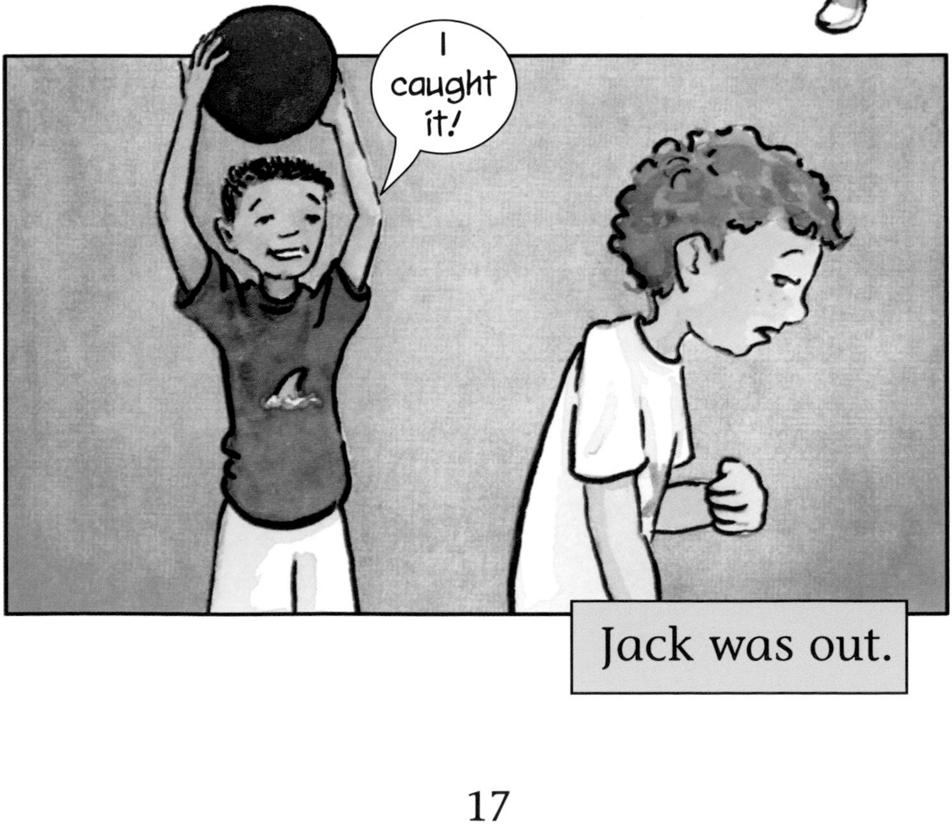
I caught it!

Jack was out.

Kyle was next. He never kicked the ball far. But he knew he could run fast.

The first ball rolled in. Kyle missed it. The second ball rolled in. Kyle missed it again. He had one more chance.

The third ball rolled in.

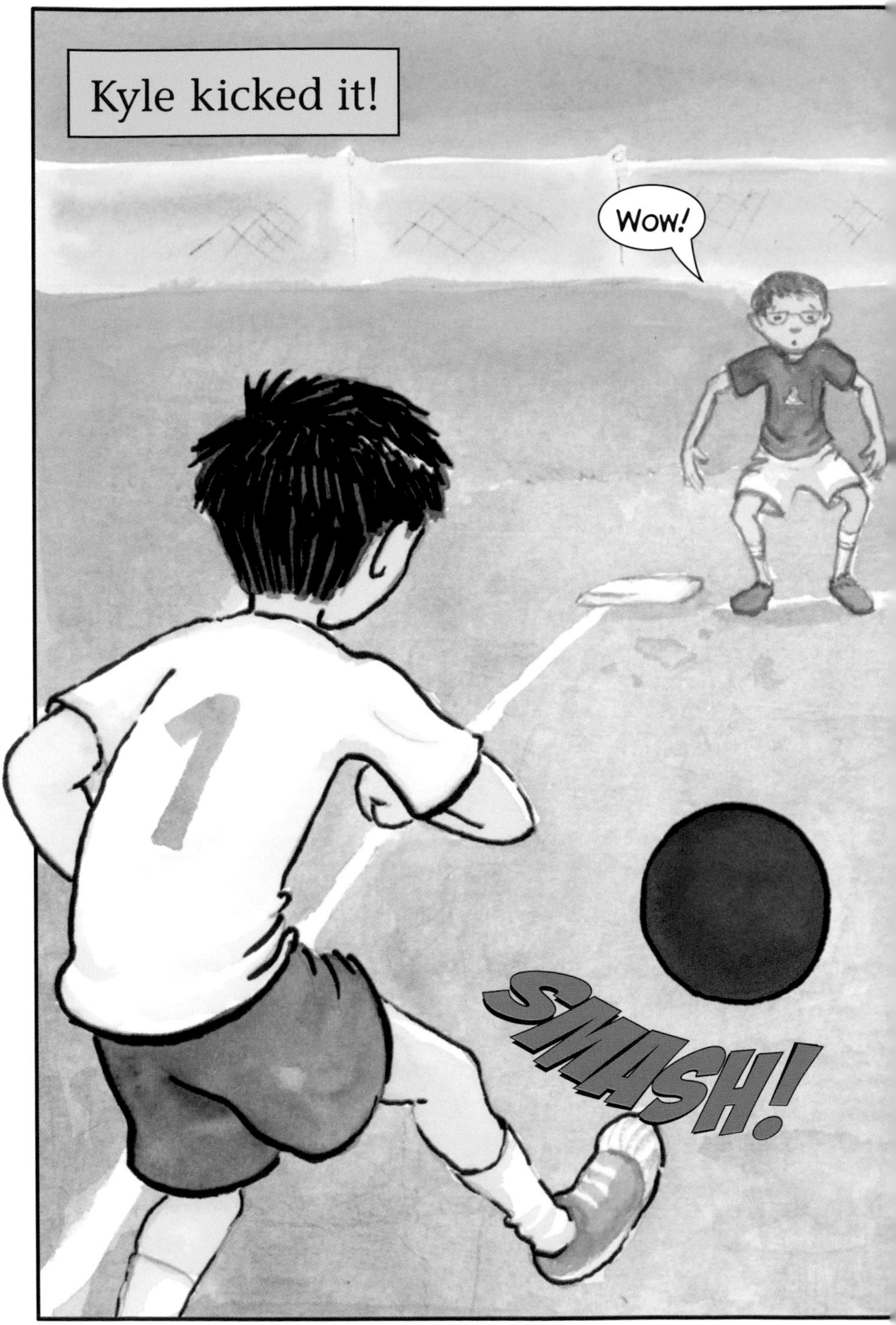
Kyle kicked it!
Wow!
SMASH!

The ball did not go far, but that was okay. Kyle was a fast runner.

Kyle ran and ran and ran.

The other team could not catch him.

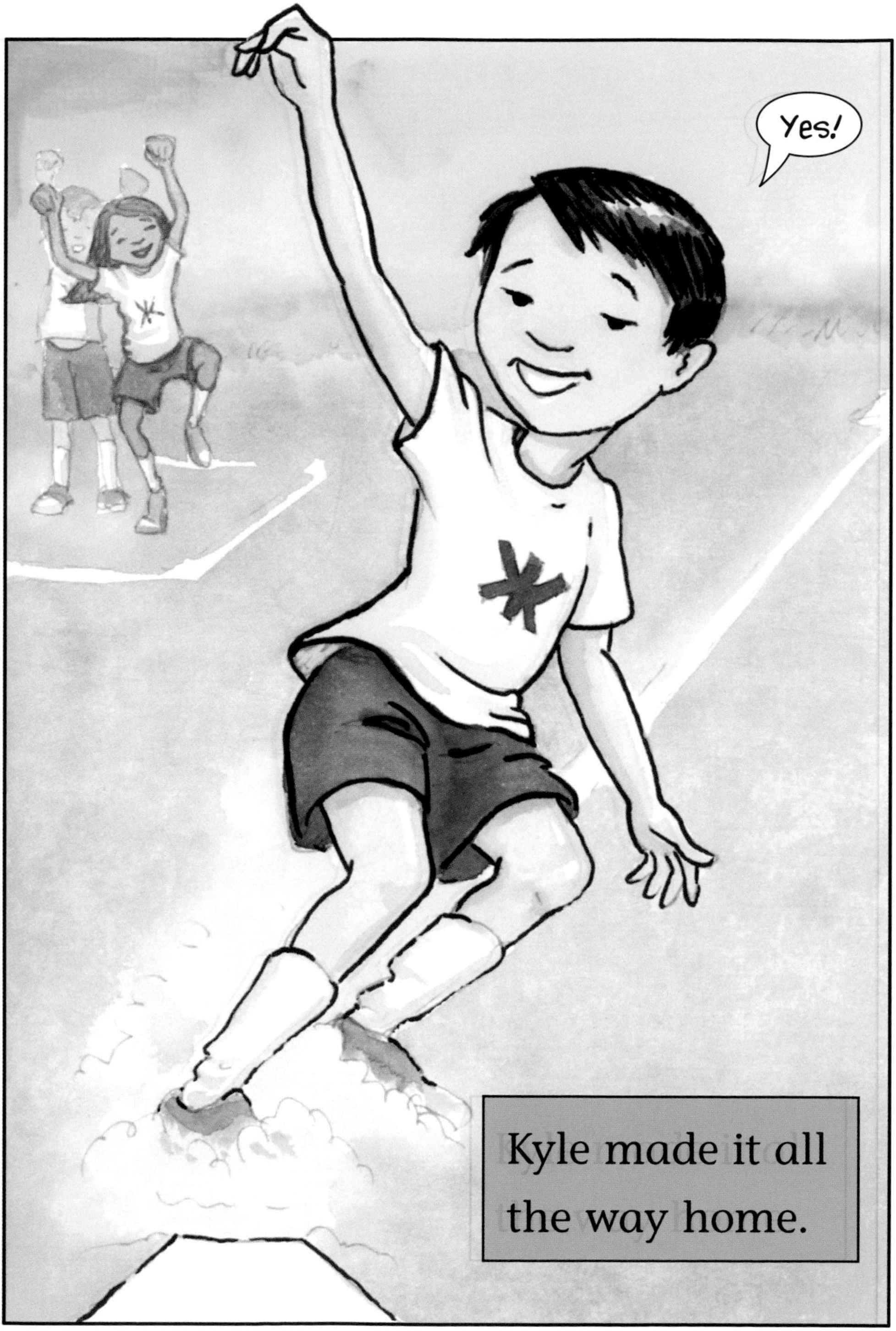
Yes!
Kyle made it all
the way home.

The Kicking Kids won the game!

And they took home the trophy.

The End

ABOUT THE AUTHOR

Cari Meister is the author of many books for children, including the My Pony Jack series and *Luther's Halloween*. She lives on a small farm in Minnesota with her husband, four sons, three horses, one dog,and one cat. Cari enjoys running, snowshoeing, horseback riding, and yoga.

ABOUT THE ILLUSTRATOR

Julie Olson grew up in the middle of six brothers and two sisters, so she learned to play kickball well. Julie found her individuality at home through art. Since then, Julie earned a BFA in illustration, illustrated numerous books for many markets, and started creating her own kickball team with a husband, two sons, and a daughter.

GLOSSARY

captain (KAP-tuhn)—the leader of the team

foul (foul)—out of bounds

inning (IN-ing)—a part of the game when one team has a turn to kick and the other team is in the outfield; then the teams switch

practice (PRAK-tiss)—to do something over and over

tournament (TUR-nuh-muhnt)—a contest with many different teams playing until one is the winner

DISCUSSION QUESTIONS

1.) Kyle and his friends loved playing kickball. What do you and your friends do together?

2.) Kyle was the captain of the kickball team. Would you like to be captain of a team? Why or why not?

3.) The Kicking Kids had to face older kids in the final game. But Kyle's team was not scared. Have you ever had to face off against older kids? Explain what happened.

WRITING PROMPTS

1.) In this book, the team names were the Kicking Kids and the Super Sharks. If you were the captain, what would you name your team? Write at least three names down.

2.) After the Kicking Kids won the big game, they got a trophy. Draw a picture of a trophy you would want to win.

3.) Throughout the book, there are sound and action words next to some of the art. Pick at least two of those words. Then write your own sentences using those words.

THE FIRST STEP INTO GRAPHIC NOVELS

My FIRST Graphic Novel

These books are the perfect introduction to the world of safe, appealing graphic novels. Each story uses familiar topics, repeating patterns, and core vocabulary words appropriate for a beginning reader. Combine the entertaining story with comic book panels, exciting action elements, and bright colors and a safe graphic novel is born.

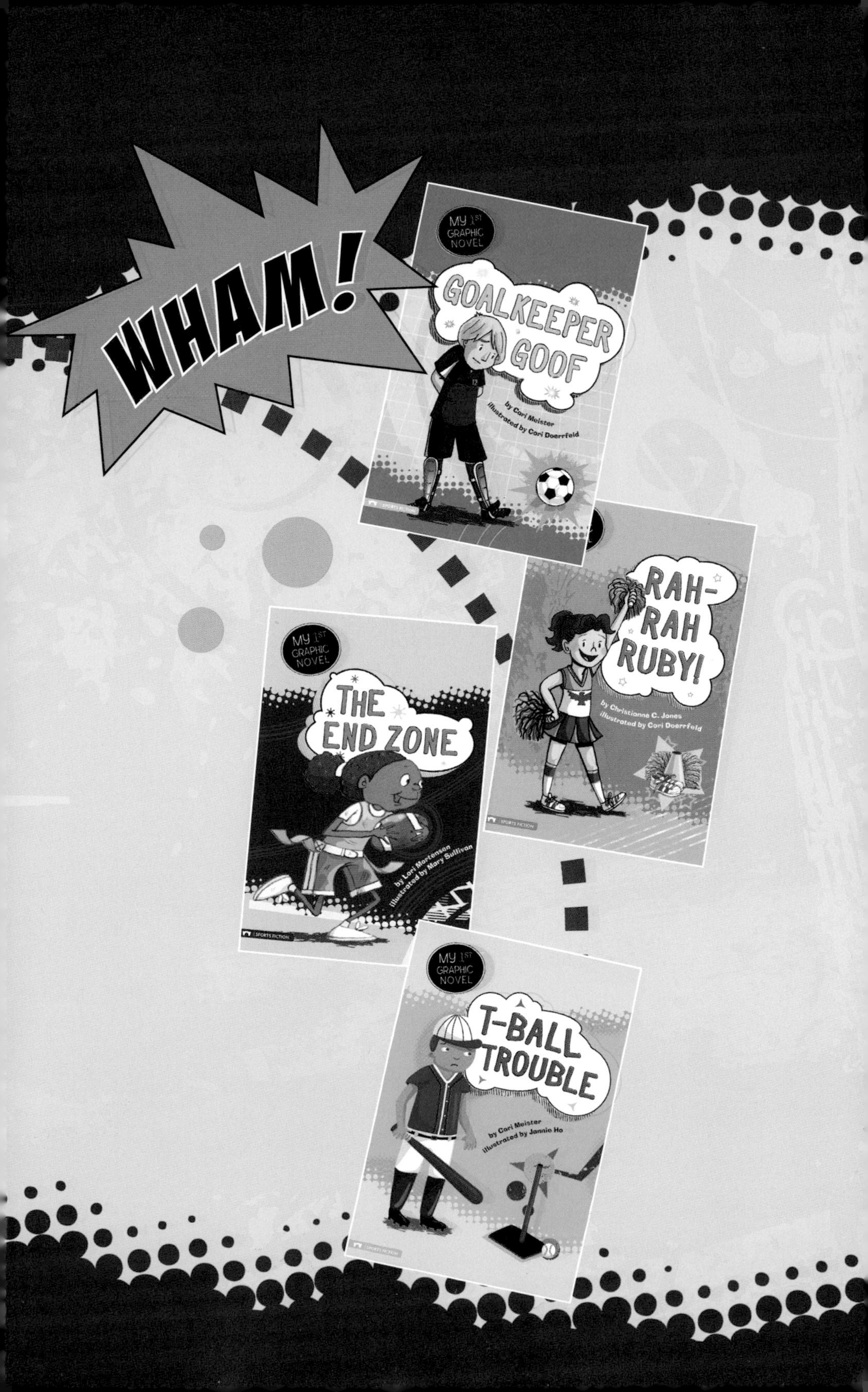
WHAM!
MY 1ST GRAPHIC NOVEL
GOALKEEPER GOOF
by Cori Meister
illustrated by Cori Doerrfeld
RAH-RAH RUBY!
by Christianne C. Jones
illustrated by Cori Doerrfeld
MY 1ST GRAPHIC NOVEL
THE END ZONE
by Lori Mortensen
illustrated by Mary Sullivan
MY 1ST GRAPHIC NOVEL
T-BALL TROUBLE
by Cori Meister
illustrated by Jannie Ho

WAIT!

DON'T CLOSE THE BOOK!

THERE'S MORE!

FIND MORE:

Games & Puzzles
Heroes & Villains
Authors & Illustrators

AT...

capstone kids.com

www.CAPSTONEKIDS.com

STILL WANT MORE?

Find cool websites and more books like this one at www.FACTHOUND.com.
Just type in the BOOK ID 1434212947 and you're ready to go!